Down at the Sea Hotel

A Greg Brown song illustrated by Mireille Levert

Dedicated to the memory of Bob Feldman,
founder of Red House Records

The tuna is tired
The seahorse is sleepy
The hammerhead's not feeling well
The catfish is yawning
It's lights-out time
Down at the Sea Hotel

They've eaten their minnows
They've eaten their worms
They have no more stories to tell
The octopus stretches
All eight of his arms
Down at the sea hotel

Good night
Sleep tight

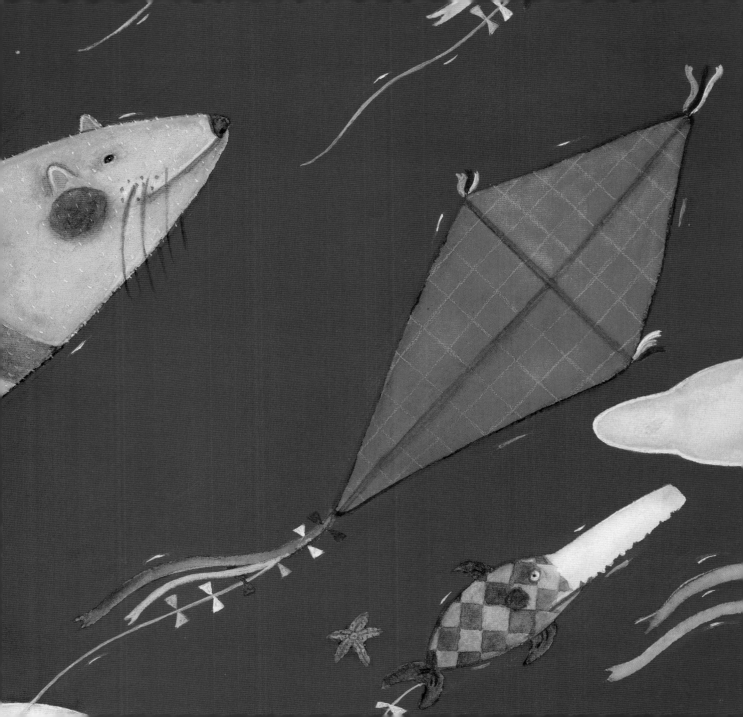

Down at the Sea Hotel

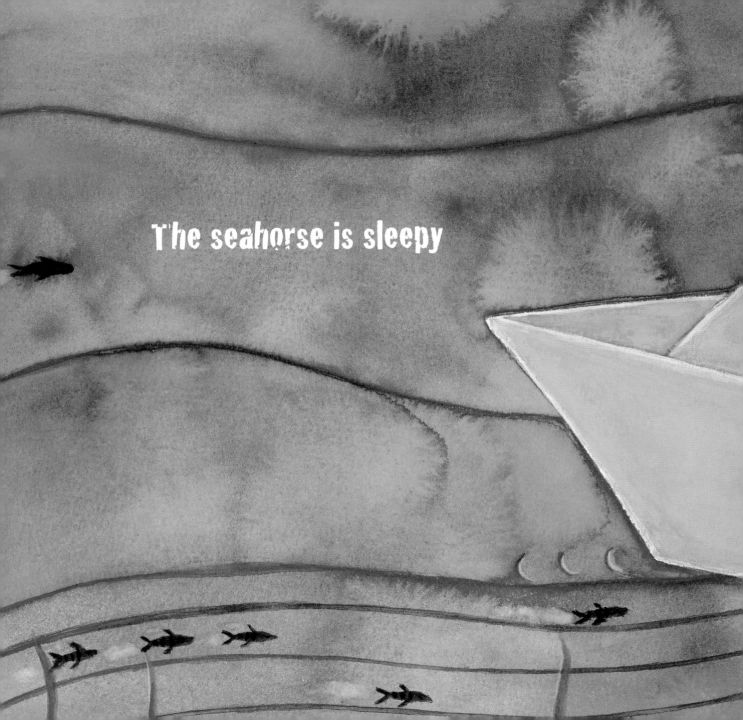

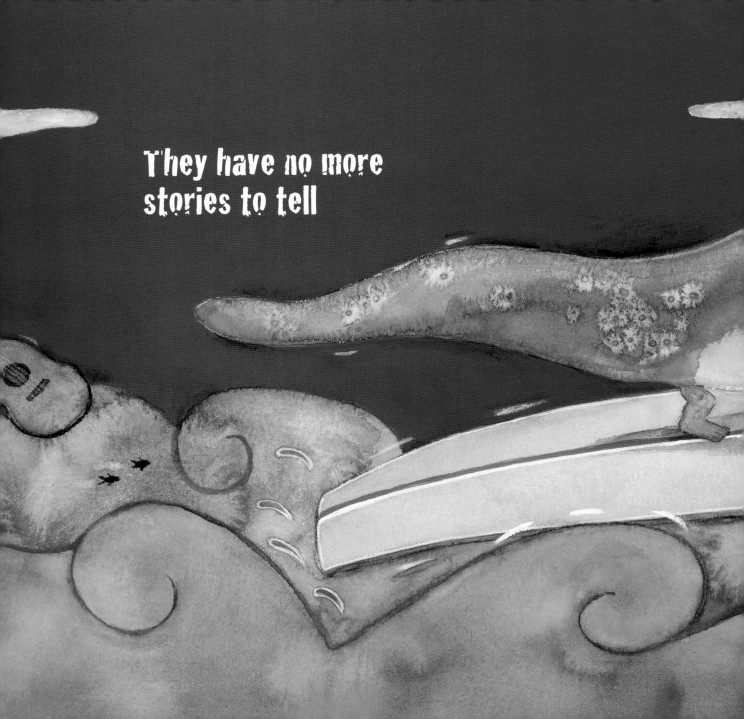

They have no more
stories to tell

Down at the Sea Hotel

Good night
Sleep tight

It's lights-out time

Down at the Sea Hotel

Down at the Sea Hotel

Singers John Gorka, Eliza Gilkyson, Lucy Kaplansky, Guy Davis, Lynn Miles and The Wailin' Jennys
(Ruth Moody, Nicky Mehta and Heather Masse) Songwriter Greg Brown (Hacklebarney Music)

The tuna is tired
The seahorse is sleepy
The hammerhead's not feeling well
The catfish is yawning
It's lights-out time
Down at the Sea Hotel

Good night
Sleep tight
Down at the Sea Hotel

They've eaten their minnows
They've eaten their worms
They have no more stories to tell
The octopus stretches
All eight of his arms
Down at the Sea Hotel

Midnight Lullaby

Singer Guy Davis
Songwriter Tom Waits (Fifth Floor Music)

Sing a song of sixpence, pocket full of rye
Hushabye my baby, no need to be crying
You can burn the midnight oil with me as long as you will
Stare out at the moon upon the windowsill, and dream...

Sing a song of sixpence, pocket full of rye
Hushabye my baby, no need to be crying
There's dew drops on the window sill and gumdrops in your head
Slipping into dream land, you're nodding your head, so dream...

Dream of West Virginia, or of the British Isles
'Cause when you are dreaming, you see for miles and miles
When you are much older, remember when we sat
At midnight on the windowsill, and had this little chat
And dream, come on and dream
Come on and dream, and dream, and dream...

Dreamland

Singer Lucy Kaplansky
Songwriter Mary Chapin Carpenter (Getarealjob Music, EMI April Music)

Sun goes down and says goodnight
Pull your covers up real tight
By your bed we'll leave a light
To guide you off to dreamland
Your pillows soft your bed is warm
Your eyes are tired when day is done
One more kiss and you'll be gone
On your way to dreamland

Every sleepy boy and girl
In every bed around the world
Can hear the stars up in the sky
Whispering a lullaby
Who knows where you'll fly away
Winging passed the light of day
The man in the moon and the Milky Way
Welcome you to dreamland

Barefoot Floors

Singers The Wailin' Jennys (Ruth Moody, Nicky Mehta and Heather Masse)
Songwriter Neil Young (Silver Fiddle Music)

Sleep, baby sleep
I know your day has been oh so long
Sleep, baby sleep
I know your day has been oh so long
The night falls at your feet
Now the day feels so complete
Compared to darkness
Sleep, baby sleep

Dream, baby dream
Sweet dreams are all it's made of
Dream, baby dream
Sweet dreams are all it's made of
Promises of the morning ways,
New beginnings for another
Day to spend together
Dream, baby dream

Love, baby love
Has got me walking on these
Barefoot floors
Love, baby love
Has got me walking on these
Barefoot floors
Find the light
Surrounding you
Sleep the night till morning's dew
I will be here for you
Love, baby love
Sleep, baby sleep

Midnight in Missoula

Singer Eliza Gilkyson
Songwriter Nanci Griffith (Ponder Heart Music, Irving Music)

Are you sleeping now?
It's midnight in Missoula
Where the Black Hills know your name
Is the snow piled high around your window frame?
Is there enough frost left to write our names upon the pane?

Are you sleeping now?
It's midnight in Missoula

I am down in Rio where I cannot find the sky
Our savior on that mountaintop has taught my soul to fly
I am singing Gershwin and children's lullabies
And wondering of you
And if you're sleeping in Missoula tonight

I'd love to climb your hilltop and look out upon Missoula lights
Sing Samuel Barber melodies with your viola sweet and high
But I am off to Liverpool on an early evening flight
And wondering of you
And if you're sleeping in Missoula tonight

Are you sleeping now?
Do you know how much I love ya?
Are you sleeping now?
It's midnight in Missoula

Do La Lay

Singer John Gorka
Songwriter Jesse Winchester (Fourth Floor Music, Hot Kitchen Music, WB Music)

Baby do la lay my child
One and one made you
So right away we make you cry
To show you who is who
Oh, little child of love
I won't get in your way
Let me look out from above
Over you baby do la lay
Oh, I am a father now

I can't get out of that
And you are my child now
You can't get out of that
Oh little child of love
I won't get in your way
Let me look out from above
Over you baby do la lay

Little Seahorse

Singer Lynn Miles
Songwriter Bruce Cockburn (Golden Mountain Music)

Little seahorse
Swimming in a primal sea
Heartbeat like a
Leaf quaking in the breeze
I feel magic as a coyote
In the middle of the moon-wild night

In the forge-fire time
Your mother glowed so bright
You were like a
Voice calling in the night
And I'm watching the curtain
Rising on a whole new set of dreams

The world is waiting
Like a Lake Superior gale
A locomotive
Racing along the rail
It'll sweep you away
But you know that you're never alone

Little seahorse
Floating on a primal tide
Quickening like a
Spark in a haystack side
I already love you
And I don't even know who you are

Goodnight, My Angel

Singer Lucy Kaplansky
Songwriter Billy Joel (Impulsive Music)

Goodnight, my angel
Time to close your eyes
And save these questions for another day
I think I know what you've been asking me
I think you know what I've been trying to say
I promised I would never leave you
And you should always know
Wherever you may go
No matter where you are
I never will be far away

Goodnight, my angel
Now it's time to sleep
And still so many things I want to say
Remember all the songs you sang for me
When we went sailing on an emerald bay
And like a boat out on the ocean
I'm rocking you to sleep
The water's dark
And deep inside this ancient heart
You'll always be a part of me

Goodnight, my angel
Now it's time to dream
And dream how wonderful your life will be
Someday your child may cry
And if you sing this lullaby
Then in your heart
There will always be a part of me

Someday we'll all be gone
But lullabies go on and on...
They never die
That's how you
And I
Will be

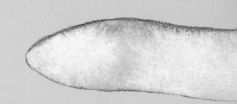

Annabel

Singer Guy Davis
Songwriters Don Henley and John Corey (Grey Hare Music)

I watch you sleeping
My weary heart rises up on wings
I hear your laughter
Something deep down inside me sings

Way down here in the land of cotton
You were born on a rainy day
Since then, sweet things long forgotten
They just keep flooding back my way

Oh child, I cannot tell you how the time just flies
But I have had my days of glory under sunny skies
These days, your bright dreams are all I want to see
Sleep tight, Annabel
You can always count on me

In this cold world, folks will judge you
Though they don't know you at all
I may not be there to catch you
Anytime that you might fall

But, you got my hard old head
And your mother's grace
All the likeness of the loved ones
Right there in your face
And I know in the end
You'll be who you will be

So sleep tight, Annabel
You can always count on me

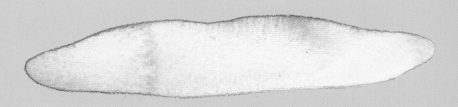

Trick Rider

Singers The Wailin' Jennys (Ruth Moody, Nicky Mehta and Heather Masse)
Songwriter Gord Downie (Wiener Art Music)

My wild child, your night light's on
You're in your mild depths
The moon is on the lawn
Just make your friends
While you're still young
Before you can't see
Through anyone

And if you're trick-riding out in the rain
Don't expect me to watch
Or ask me to explain

I'll be your friend, your last refuge
When things get weird
And weird breaks huge
I'll stroke your hair
I'll dry your cheeks
When failures come
And no one speaks

But if you're on a horse
Trick-riding in the mud and rain
You can't expect me to watch
Or ask me to explain

Everybody Cries

Singer Lynn Miles
Songwriter Jim Cuddy (Buried Crow Music)

Close your eyes my dear
There's no need to wake
We all get tired from the
Chances that we take
I wish that I could take away
The tears from your eyes it's just that
Sometimes everybody cries

Outside the walls around us
You must be strong
And when you feel you're walking
All alone
Just remember I'll be there
To greet you when you rise it's okay
Sometimes everybody cries

I've seen you watching people
Walking through this world
Seeing what they do to try
To make it through each day
Don't be alarmed there's something
Out there waiting just for you someday

Let the stars fall down
Over your head
And don't you worry about
The things you said
Just you drift away into
The world behind your eyes it's okay
Sometimes everybody cries
Sometimes everybody cries

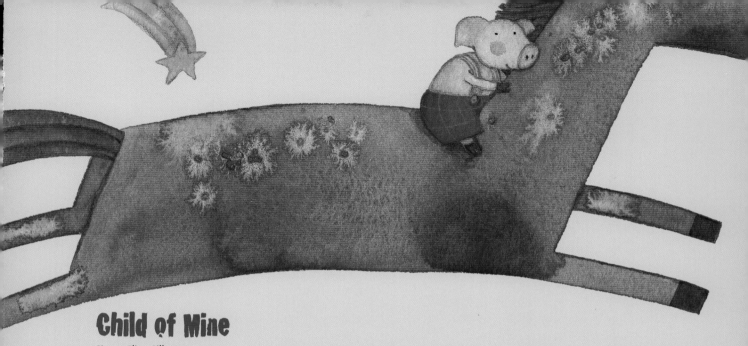

Child of Mine

Singer Eliza Gilkyson
Songwriters Carole King and Gerald Goffin (Screen Gems – EMI Music)
Back-up vocals Hart-Rouge (Michelle, Suzanne and Paul Campagne)

Although you see the world
Different than me
Sometimes I can touch upon
The wonders that you see
And all the new colors
And pictures you've designed
Oh yes, sweet darling
So glad you are a child of mine

Child of mine, child of mine
Oh yes, sweet darling
So glad you are a child of mine

You don't need direction
You know which way to go
And I don't want to hold you back
I just want to watch you grow

And you're the one who taught me
You don't have to look behind

Nobody's gonna kill your dreams
Or tell you how to live your life
There'll always be people
Who make it hard for a while
But you'll turn their heads
When they see you smile

The times you were born in
May not have been the best
But you can make the times to come
Better than the rest
I know you will be honest
If you can't always be kind

Things We've Handed Down

Singer John Gorka
Songwriter Marc Cohn (Famous Music)

Don't know much about you
Don't know who you are
We've been doing fine without you
But, we could only go so far
Don't know why you chose us
Were you watching from above
Is there someone there that knows us
Said we'd give you all our love

Will you laugh just like your mother
Will you sigh like your old man
Some things skip a generation
Like I've heard they often can
Are you a poet or a dancer
A devil or a clown
Or a strange new combination of
The things we've handed down

I wonder who you'll look like
Will your hair fall down in curls
Will you be a mama's boy
Or daddy's little girl
Will you be a sad reminder
Of what's been lost along the way

Maybe you can help me find her
In the things you do and say

And these things that we have given you
They are not so easily found
But you can thank us later
For the things we've handed down

You may not always be so grateful
For the way that you were made
Some feature of your father's
That you'd gladly sell or trade
And one day you may look at us
And say that you were cursed
But over time that line has been
Extremely well rehearsed
By our fathers, and their fathers
In some old and distant town
From the places no one here remembers
Come the things we've handed down

Nothing But a Child

Singers John Gorka, Eliza Gilkyson, Lucy Kaplansky, Guy Davis, Lynn Miles and The Wailin' Jennys (Ruth Moody, Nicky Mehta and Heather Masse) Songwriter Steve Earle (Goldmine Music)

Once upon a time in a far off land
Wise men saw a sign and set out across the sand
Songs of praise to sing, they traveled day and night
And precious gifts to bring, guided by the light

They chased a brand new star, ever towards the west
Across the mountains far, but when it came to rest
They scarce believed their eyes, they'd come so many miles
And this miracle they prized was nothing but a child

Nothing but a child could wash those tears away
Or guide a weary world into the light of day
And nothing but a child could help erase those miles
So once again we all can be children for a while

Now all around the world, in every little town
Every day is heard a precious little sound
And every mother kind and every father proud
Looks down in awe to find another chance allowed

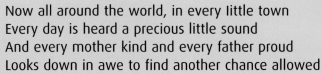

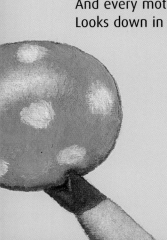

John Gorka, Eliza Gilkyson, Lucy Kaplansky and Guy Davis appear courtesy of Red House Records
Lynn Miles appears courtesy of Red House Records and True North Records
The Wailin' Jennys appear courtesy of Red House Records and Jericho Beach Music

Record Producer Paul Campagne Artistic Director Roland Stringer Illustrations Mireille Levert
Design Stephan Lorti for Haus Design Communications Recorded by Paul Campagne at Studio King, Montreal
Except Stephanie Labbé at Dogger Pond Music, Lucy Kaplansky at Kampo Studios, New York NY (with Alan Ford),
Eliza Gilkyson at Congress House Studios, Austin TX (with Mark Hallman), and John Gorka at By The Dog, Marine, MN
Mixed and mastered by Davy Gallant and Paul Campagne at Dogger Pond Music

Musicians Paul Campagne acoustic, electric and classical guitar, electric and upright bass, percussions
Davy Gallant drums, mandolin, percussions, electric and acoustic guitar, flute Steve Normandin piano, accordion
Stéphanie Labbé violin Rick Haworth slide guitar, dobro Guy Davis acoustic guitar, harmonica (Midnight Lullaby)
Gilles Tessier electric guitar (Annabel, Everybody Cries) Jeremy Penner mandolin (Barefoot Floors), violin (Trick Rider)
Heather Masse upright bass (Trick Rider, Barefoot Floors) Ruth Moody acoustic guitar (Trick Rider), accordion (Barefoot Floors)
Nicky Mehta acoustic guitar (Barefoot Floors), ukulele (Trick Rider)

Thank you to Beth Friend, Eric Peltoniemi, Chris Frymire, Jack Schuller, Thom Wolke,
Bernie Finkelstein and David Tamulevich.

We acknowledge the financial support of the Government of Canada through the Canada Music Fund for this project.
A part of the proceeds from the sale of this album will be donated to the Breast Cancer Fund.

ISBN-10: 2-923163-34-6 / ISBN-13: 978-2-923163-34-5
℗© 2007 Folle Avoine Productions ⓦwww.thesecretmountain.com